MW01273861

*To love for the sake of being*

*loved is human,*

*But to love for the sake of*

*loving is angelic.*

To Tim

Dream On

Brethren

*Benned*

Alphonse Marie Louis de Lamartine (1790-1869) French romantic poet

# Guardian

# Angels

We are all children of the Universe. Searching, feeling and experiencing our lives on our individual journeys. We are free yet bound, aware yet vulnerable. We are human beings who are complex, loveable and dynamic, and yet sometimes unaware that we need to draw our strength from a deeper level.

Guardian Angels are with us. They are wholesome entities of the purest intention. Non-judgemental and protective, they are always there, guiding us from another dimension.

Guardian Angels emanate a truth beyond expression. Their message is to encourage humanity to live a life of peace, growth and love.

My spiritual journey, extensive travels and love of Angels have come together to inspire me to create and photograph Angels of my own. All the people who appear in my images are friends and family who freely volunteered their time. I believe my Guardian Angels helped me connect with these people. In my book I celebrate them and thank them for their participation, support and love.

After many years of specialising in photographing Angels, I welcome you to enjoy the best of my creative work, complemented by powerful quotes spoken by legendary people from all walks of life. People who made a difference, and through their enduring words have changed the way we live, love and perceive.

I hope this book makes a difference to you.

Bernard Rosa.

Only those who attempt the absurd...

will achieve the impossible.

I think...I think it's in my basement...

Let me go upstairs and check.

Mauritis Escher (1898-1972) Dutch artist

Be fully in the moment,

open yourself to the powerful energies

dancing around you.

Ernest Miller Hemingway (1899-1961) American writer

When one door closes another door opens;

but we so often look so long

and so regretfully upon the closed door,

that we do not see the ones which open for us.

Alexander Graham Bell (1847-1922) American inventor, telephone pioneer

I like to be a free spirit.

Some don't like that,

but that's the way I am.

Princess Diana (1961-2001)British Royalty

To be wronged is nothing unless

you continue to remember it.

Confucius (c. 551-479? BC) Chinese sage

Think like a queen.

A queen is not afraid to fail.

Failure is

another steppingstone to greatness.

Oprah Winfrey (b. 1954) American talk show host

A dog is the only thing on earth

that loves you

more than you love yourself.

Josh Billings (1818-85) American humorist

A musician must make music,

an artist must paint,

a poet must write if he is to be ultimately

at peace with himself. What one can be,

one must be.

Abraham Maslow (1908-1970) American psychologist

Loving someone deeply gives you strength.

Being loved

by someone deeply gives you courage.

Lao-Tzu (6th century B.C.) Legendary Chinese philosopher

What you spend years building

may be destroyed overnight.

Build anyway.

Mother Teresa (1910-1997) Albanian-born Indian nun

Do not go where the path may lead.

Go instead

where there is no path and leave a trail.

Ralph Waldo Emerson (1803-1882) American writer, philosopher, poet

Real friendship

is shown in times of trouble;

prosperity is full of friends.

Euripides (480?-406 BC)  Greek dramatist

Until he extends his circle of compassion

to include all living things,

man will not himself find peace.

Albert Schweitzer (1875-1965)  French philosopher, physician, musician

The basic difference between

an ordinary person and a warrior

is that a warrior takes everything as a challenge

while an ordinary person takes everything

as a blessing or a curse.

Carlos Castaneda (1925-1998) American writer

There are two ways of spreading light;

to be the candle

or the mirror that reflects it.

Edith Newbold Jones Wharton (1862-1937) American writer

The secret of health for both mind and body

is not to mourn for the past,

not to worry about the future,

or not to anticipate troubles,

but to live in the present moment

wisely and earnestly.

Buddha (563?-483? BC) Indian mystic

You cannot teach a man anything;

you can only

help him find it within himself.

Galileo Galilei (1564-1642) Italian astronomer

The peace of heaven

is theirs that lift their swords,

in such a just an charitable war.

William Shakespeare (1564-1616) English playwright, poet

When choosing between two evils,

I always like to try the one

I've never tried before.

Mae West (1892-1980) American actress

I offer you peace. I offer you love.

I offer you friendship. I see your beauty.

I hear your need. I feel your feelings.

My wisdom flows from the Highest Source.

I salute that Source in you.

Let us work together for unity and love.

Mohandas Gandhi (1869-1948) India spiritual leader

If I have seen further...

it is by

standing upon the shoulders of giants.

*Sir Isaac Newton (1642-1727) English mathematician, scientist*

Friendship is...

the sort of love

one can imagine between angels.

Clive Staples Lewis (1898-1963) British writer "The Chronicles of Narnia"

Few will have the greatness to bend history itself;

but each of us can work to change

a small portion of events, and in the total;

of all those acts will be written

the history of this generation.

Robert Francis Kennedy (1925-1968) US Attorney General

Once you have flown,

you will walk the earth

with your eyes turned skyward;

for there you have been,

there you long to return.

Leonardo da Vinci (1452-1519)Italian artist.inrentor

If you don't like something change it.

If you can't change it,

change your attitude.

Don't complain.

Maya Angelou (b. 1928) American author, poet laureate

The greatest glory

in living

lies not in never falling,

but in rising

every time we fall.

Nelson Mandela (b. 1918) South African political leader

Parents can only give good advice

or put them on the right paths,

but the final forming of a person's

character lies in their own hands.

Anne Frank (1929-1945) German Jewish refugee,

For it was not into my ear

you whispered,

but into my heart.

It was not my lips you kissed,

but my soul.

Judy Garland (1922-1969) American actress

From your parents you learn love and laughter

and how to put one

foot before the other.

But when books are opened

you discover

that you have wings.

Helen Hayes (1900-1993) American actress, Academy Award winner

I saw the angel

in the marble

and carved until I set him free.

Buonarroti Michelangelo (1475-1564) Italian sculptor, painter, poet

The man who has no imagination

has no wings.

Muhammad Ali (b. 1942) American prizefighter

It is good to realize

that if love and peace can prevail on earth,

and if we can teach our children

to honor nature's gifts,

the joys and beauties of the outdoors

will be here forever.

James Earl "Jimmy" Carter, Jr. (b. 1924)  39th US President

How can you buy or sell the sky,

the warmth of the land?

The idea is strange to us.

If we do not own the freshness of the air

and the sparkle of the water,

how can you buy them?

Every part of the earth is sacred to my people.

*Chief Seattle (c. 1784-1866) Chief of the Duwamish*

I have learned

not to worry about love;

but to honor its coming with all my heart.

Alice Walker (b. 1944)  American writer

Like the winds of the sea

are the winds of fate

As we voyage along through life,

Tis the set of the soul

That decides its goal

And not the calm or the strife.

Ella Wheeler Wilcox (1850-1919) American writer, poet

Few men

have the natural strength

to honour a friend's success without envy.

Eschylus (525-456 BC) Greek tragic dramatist

Count him braver

who overcomes his desires

than him who conquers his enemies,

for the hardest

victory is over self."

Aristotle (384-322 BC) Greek philosopher

We are all visitors to this time,

this place.

We are just passing through.

Our purpose here is to observe,

to learn, to grow, to love...

and then we return home.

Australian Aboriginal Proverb

Your body is precious.

It is our vehicle

for awakening.

Treat it with care.

Buddha (563?-483? BC), Indian mystic

We are all in the gutter,

but some of

us are looking at the stars.

Oscar Wilde (1854-1900) Irish writer, playwright

Let us be grateful to people

who make us happy;

they are the

charming gardeners

who make our souls blossom.

Marcel Proust (1871-1922) French writer

Be kind,

for everyone you meet

is fighting a hard battle.

Plato (427?-347? BC) Greek philosopher

I have sometimes been wildly,

despairingly,

acutely miserable ...

but through it all I still know quite certainly

that just to be alive

is a grand thing.

Agatha Christie (1891-1976) British mystery writer

We have all been given free will.

And the direction

we choose

to go is up to us...

Theodore Roosevelt (1858-1919) 26th US President

Dream lofty dreams, and as you dream,

so you shall become.

Your vision is the promise

of what you shall one day be;

your ideal is the prophecy of what

you shall at last unveil.

James Lane Allen (1849-1923) American novelist

Kind hearts are the garden

Kind thoughts are the roots

Kind words are the flowers,

Kind deeds are the fruits.

Take care of your garden

And keep out the weeds,

Fill it with sunshine

Kind words and kind deeds.

Henry Wadsworth Longfellow (1807-1882) American writer, poet

I am enough of an artist

to draw freely upon my imagination.

Imagination is more important than knowledge.

Knowledge is limited.

Imagination encircles the world.

Albert Einstein (1875-1955) German-born American theoretical physicist

The best and safest thing

is to keep a balance in your life,

acknowledge the great powers

around us and in us.

If you can do that, and live that way,

you are really a wise man.

Euripides (480?-406 BC) Greek dramatist

As you think, you travel,

and as you love, you attract.

You are today where your thoughts

have brought you;

you will be tomorrow where

your thoughts take you.

James Lane Allen (1849-1923) American novelist

www.bernardrosa.com

## Special Thanks

My mum Fay

Natasha Kogan

Georgie Jeffrey

Janine Fuller

Piers Fisher-Pollard

Pete Carette

Gary Allen

ISBN 1-920970-02-9

© 2004 Original images - Bernard Rosa

© 2004 Concept, design, format and photography – Bernard Rosa

© Published in 2004 By The Great Work Publishing

www.the-great-work.com

Printed in China at Everbest Printing Company.

"What is man without the beasts?

If all the beasts were gone,

man would die from a great loneliness of spirit.

For whatever happens to the beasts,

soon happens to man.

All things are connected."

Chief Seattle (c. 1784-1866) Chief of the Duwamish, Suquamish and allied Indian tribes